A Walk Through the Woods

A Walk Through the Woods

by May Sarton

Pictures by Kazue Mizumura

Harper & Row, Publishers
New York, Evanston, San Francisco, London

A WALK THROUGH THE WOODS
Text copyright © 1976 by May Sarton
Illustrations copyright © 1976 by Kazue Mizumura
All rights reserved. No part of this book may be used or
reproduced in any manner whatsoever without written permission
except in the case of brief quotations embodied in critical
articles and reviews. Printed in the United States of America.
For information address Harper & Row, Publishers, Inc.,
10 East 53rd Street, New York, N.Y. 10022. Published simultaneously
in Canada by Fitzhenry & Whiteside Limited, Toronto.
Library of Congress Catalog Card Number: 75-25413
Trade ISBN 0-06-025189-1
Harpercrest ISBN 0-06-025190-5
FIRST EDITION

For Mary Leigh
whose woods these are

All morning
we are apart

Lazy Tamas
snoozing in his bed

Bramble
out hunting
since dawn

I at my desk
making up poems.

About noon
we are suddenly restless.
"Where is she?"
Tamas wonders.
"Time for a walk."
He gets up and stretches.

"Time for a walk,"
thinks Bramble
sitting up
on the terrace wall.

I run downstairs
and put on my coat.
"Come on, everybody,
it's time for a walk!"

Tamas races
round and round—
"Speed!" he barks.
"Speed is what I need!"

Bramble makes a fat tail
as he goes by.
She stands still
till things calm down.
"A walk," she thinks,
"is a quiet thing.

"Don't wait for me.
I'll be along,
wild and alone,
in my own good time."

Tamas slows down
for the morning news.
He is told by his nose
a skunk passed by
in the night.

A pheasant crossed the road
early this morning.
He trots briskly
behind his nose.

The real walk begins.
I follow Tamas.
Bramble follows me.
She likes to be near us
but not too near.

Sometimes she decides
to catch up.
Her tail goes up like a flag.
She rubs against my legs.
I can feel her purrs.

We are glad
to be together
walking the wild woods
on a spring day.

I hurry to see
whether the lady-slipper
has come out
under the big pine.

Tamas stands still.
His ears are pricked.
He rushes into a thicket
and flushes a woodcock.
He barks his surprise.

Bramble runs up a tree
just for the fun of it.

I think I see the lady-slipper...
yes, there it is,
a secret treasure.

We are each absorbed
in looking
and listening
and smelling
the spring smells,
woodsy and mossy
and wet.

A squirrel
teases Bramble
from a high branch,
and she miaows.

Tamas finds hoof marks.
He runs up and down
and round and round
barking sharp barks,
"Deer! Deer! Deer
have been here!"

I pick up
an emerald cushion
of moss.
It feels like velvet.

Then we come to
the big field.
Tamas rolls on his back
in the fresh grass.

Bramble pounces on
something so tiny
only she knows it is there.

I stand still
in the warm sun.

Then we are on our way
home past the swamp
where warblers are warbling
and a towhee
gives a sharp cry.

We are under the beech trees.
Their sharp green leaves
have just unfurled.
It is darker here.

And now we come out
at our own gates.
We have made a circle.

Tamas has to run
and bark again.
"Speed!" he barks.
"Speed is what I need."

Bramble makes a fat tail
and leaps into the air
as he goes by.

"I think I'll stay here,
wild and alone."
But she changes her mind.

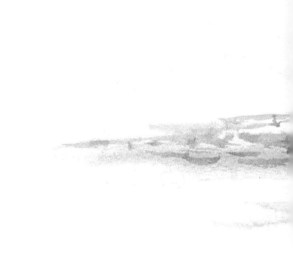

And
we all run home.

Time for lunch
a saucer of cream
a crisp dry bone
bread and cheese
and a nap for us all.
Even the birds
are resting now
in the lovely woods.